Autumn is for Apples

By **Michelle Knudsen**

Illustrated by
Denise and Fernando

A Random House PICTUREBACK® Shape Book

Random House 🏠 New York

Text copyright © 2001 by Michelle Knudsen. Illustrations copyright © 2001 by Denise and Fernando.
All rights reserved under International and Pan-American Copyright Conventions.
Published in the United States by Random House, Inc., New York,
and simultaneously in Canada by Random House of Canada Limited, Toronto.

www.randomhouse.com/kids

Library of Congress Cataloging-in-Public
Knudsen, Michelle.
Autumn is for apples / by Michelle Knudsen ; illustrated by Denise and Fernand
Summary: When the weather turns cool and crisp, a family visits an apple orchard and savors the crunchy sweetness of freshly picked apples.
ISBN: 0-375-81090-0 [1. Apples—Fiction. 2. Autumn—Fiction. 3. Stories in rhyme.] I. Denise, ill. II. Fernando, ill. III. Title.
IV. Random House pictureback. PZ8.3.K75115 Au 2001 [E]—dc21 00-046886
Printed in the United States of America July 2001 10 9 8 7 6 5 4 3 2
PICTUREBACK, RANDOM HOUSE, and the Random House colophon are registered trademarks of Random House, Inc.

Autumn is for apples.
It's my favorite time of year.
The air is crisp but not too cold.
The sky is bright and clear.

And every new September,
I count the days until
we go to pick some apples
from the orchard on the hill.

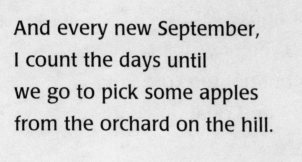

Daddy hauls the ladder
and my brother brings a sack.
I grab my hat and glove and ball
and race him out the back.

Mother brings a picnic lunch,
all neatly packed away.
And then we pile into the car
and start upon our way.

And when the blacktop turns to earth,
Dad parks along the side.
The orchard opens leafy arms
and welcomes us inside.

MACK'S APPLE
ORCHARD
YOU PICK 'EM!

And then—hooray!—it's picking time.
My brother climbs a tree.
He plucks an apple from a branch
and throws it down to me.

The orchard road's a winding one
with lots of twists and bends.
I know the roadside trees so well
they've all become my friends.

We climb and pick and pick some more
until it's time for lunch.
Mother hands out sandwiches.
We chatter as we munch.

We run and toss the ball around
until it's time to go.
But I know that we'll be back again
before the winter snow.

Apples are my favorite snack—
so juicy, red, and round.
I love how every tasty bite
comes with a crunchy sound.

They're good in pies and apple tarts
or sliced and served with tea.
My favorite kinds of apples, though,
are those straight from the tree.

8279201

Autumn is for apples—
and apples are for me!